The BIG Haunted House Book

If you enjoy The Big Haunted House Book,
then you'll love these three huge collections
of fantastic stories:

The Big Magic Animal Book
The Marmalade Pony *by Linda Newbery*
Mr Wellington Boots *by Ann Ruffell*
The Wishing Horse *by Malcolm Yorke*

The Big Book of Dragons
The Little Pet Dragon *by Philippa Gregory*
School for Dragons *by Ann Jungman*
The Bad-Tempered Dragon *by Joan Lennon*

The Big Wicked Witch Book
Fisherwitch *by Susan Gates*
Broomstick Services *by Ann Jungman*
The Cleaning Witch *by Cecilia Lenagh*

The BIG Haunted House Book

Spooky Movie
CLAIRE RONAN

Bumps in the Night
FRANK RODGERS

Scarem's House
MALCOLM YORKE

Hippo

Scholastic Children's Books,
Commonwealth House, 1–19 New Oxford Street,
London WC1A 1NU, UK
a division of Scholastic Ltd
London ~ New York ~ Toronto ~ Sydney ~ Auckland

Published in this edition by Scholastic Ltd, 1998

Spooky Movie
First published in the UK by Scholastic Ltd, 1997
Text copyright © Claire Ronan, 1997
Illustrations copyright © Sami Sweeten, 1997

Bumps in the Night
First published in the UK by Scholastic Ltd, 1996
Text copyright © Frank Rodgers, 1996
Illustrations copyright © Philip Hopman, 1996

Scarem's House
First published in the UK by Scholastic Ltd, 1994
Text copyright © Malcolm Yorke, 1994
Illustrations copyright © Terry McKenna, 1994

Cover illustration copyright © Tania Hurt-Newton, 1998

ISBN 0 590 54356 3

Typeset by M Rules
Printed by WSOY, Finland

2 4 6 8 10 9 7 5 3 1

Contents

Spooky Movie

CLAIRE RONAN

Illustrated by Sami Sweeten

For Michael, Jane, Tom,
Sandy & Sam Ronan,
With Love

Chapter 1

The Birthday Present

Dexter was tall and skinny with a mess of black hair that stuck up like a toothbrush. He was one night away from being ten years old.

Every year on his birthday, Dexter travelled to Scotland to visit his Uncle Igor, who lived in a huge crumbly castle on the edge of a cliff.

Dexter loved visiting his uncle – it was always exciting.

When he woke up next morning, Dexter gobbled down his breakfast,

blew out the candles on his birthday
cake, ripped open his presents, then

travelled up to Scotland.

As he looked out of the train window the houses became green fields, then the green fields became grey moors, then the grey moors became rocks and mountains covered in swirls of mist. At last Dexter arrived at Uncle Igor's castle.

Gargoyles goggled at him from the battlements, old weeds and dandelions waggled their shaggy heads from cracks in the tumbledown walls.

Dexter looked about him. The castle was deserted, as always. Then, for a second, Dexter thought he saw a face gazing out of one of the pointy windows.

Dexter plonked down his suitcase and tapped at the studded oak door.

As he stood and waited, he heard Uncle Igor's footsteps slap, slap, slap down the stone steps of the castle's staircase. The door creaked open on rusty hinges, and his uncle's long bony face poked round. His round brown eyes peered at Dexter from below a black velvet hat like a crushed mushroom.

"Dexter! My dear young fellow, many happy returns of the day!" he cried. "Glad your mum let you stay for a couple of days. Sorry the butler wasn't here to open the door for you, eh! What?"

"Have you remembered my birthday present?" said Dexter hopefully.

"Wouldn't forget an important thing like that! I've hidden it somewhere."

Uncle Igor started fiddling with the folds of his black velvet cloak. Then he cried, "Ah ha! Gotcha!" and handed Dexter a brown paper parcel.

"Feels heavy," said Dexter, peering at the squiggly writing on the top.

It said —

Dexter knew that only one person in the whole world had writing as terrible as that: Uncle Igor's butler, Jeffreys.

"Jeffreys wrote that, didn't he?" said Dexter.

"Yes! He's a total nincompoop! Couldn't spell if his life depended on it!" spluttered Uncle Igor.

11

"But Jeffreys must be more than a hundred," said Dexter.

"Jeffreys is only the butler, we don't bother to count his birthdays! He's whinged on all day because a gargoyle toppled off the battlements and flattened that smelly old cat of his.

Silly old fool is still in his bedroom, snivelling and dabbing his nose with a soaking wet hanky."

"I saw him looking down from one of the top windows," said Dexter.

"What are you talking about? Jeffreys' bedroom is in the dungeon. He hasn't got any windows!" said Uncle Igor.

A shivery tingle ran down Dexter's spine. Nobody else lived in the castle.

Perhaps he'd seen a ghost? He'd better not say any more about it. He didn't want to frighten Uncle Igor.

"I'm sorry to hear Jeffreys' cat's been squashed. What a shame," he said.

"What about *me?*" shouted Uncle Igor, waggling his bony finger under Dexter's nose. "He didn't serve my chocolate biscuits until gone three!

Disgraceful conduct, eh! What? Stop gossiping about him and open your present."

Dexter unknotted the string and tore off the brown paper. "Wow!" he gasped.

"Is it better than the presents your mum gave you?" asked Uncle Igor.

"She gave me glow-in-the-dark stars for my bedroom ceiling and some coloured pencils."

"Not as good as this, eh! What?"

"No way! It's fantastic! It's great! It's the best present I've ever had! . . . What is it?"

Chapter 2

The Video Camera

"It's a video camera, you numbskull!" cried Uncle Igor. "I thought you could make a film in the castle!"

"I could go up to the top of the battlements and film the sea crashing against the rocks below," said Dexter.

"Don't be so boring! I'll help you make a proper film with a star-studded cast," said Uncle Igor. He took off his crushed mushroom hat, smoothed his silvery hair and twirled the ends of his curly white moustache.

"But we don't know any stars," said Dexter.

"I'm going to star in your film myself!" said Uncle Igor. "We'll have a bite to eat first – this filming business is going to be hard work, and we need to get our strength up, eh! What?"

Uncle Igor and Dexter trooped along miles of draughty passageways, marched through room after room with cobwebby corners, and climbed dozens of twisty stone staircases. At last they reached the dining room. They sat down at each end of a long, polished table.

"Come along, Jeffreys!" yelled Uncle Igor. "We want our dinner! Don't dilly-dally! Don't shilly-shally! Get a move on!"

Dexter heard a pair of boots clomp, clomp, clomp along the passageway, then Jeffreys plodded into the room carrying a large silver soup bowl.

His face was as crumbly as old Christmas cake, and his tiny dark eyes had wrinkles all around them, like a tortoise's. They were red from crying.

"About time too! Still snivelling, I see, Jeffreys. Your suit's got baked beans squashed down the front, your bow-tie's a knot instead of a bow, and how many times have I got to tell you that butlers aren't supposed to wear Dr Martens boots with their uniforms!"

"Sorry, sir," croaked Jeffreys. "It's my poor feet, they're not what they used to be. I've got bunions something chronic."

"What's that? Onions? I don't want any onions! I ordered tomato soup today!" shouted Uncle Igor.

Jeffreys plonked down the soup bowl. A large tear splashed down his cheek. "I'm sorry, sir," he croaked. "It's Hector, my poor cat! I don't know what I'm going to do without him, he was such a good old friend to me!"

Dexter leant across the table and squeezed Jeffreys' knobbly hand. "I'm sorry, Jeffreys," he said.

Another tear dripped off the end of Jeffreys' nose. "He used to sit on my lap," he sobbed, "in front of the fire and purr, he —"

A loud buzzing noise filled the dining room. It was like the sound a gigantic bumble-bee might make. Dexter looked at Uncle Igor, and saw he'd fallen asleep and started snoring.

At that moment the room lit up with yellow lightning; a split-second later a clap of thunder exploded outside. Uncle Igor woke up with a start.

"Good grief!" he yelled, jumping up from his chair and knocking over the soup. "Jumping jackrabbits! Did you hear that? Tonight's the night to film, Dexter, my lad!"

"What's so special about tonight, Uncle?" said Dexter.

Uncle Igor's eyes looked like two golf balls about to burst. "There's a thunderstorm, you ninny! Don't you know what that means?"

"No," said Dexter.

"It means the ghost of Lady Grizel will stalk the castle at the stroke of midnight. You said you saw her once, didn't you, Jeffreys?"

"I did indeed, sir. Turned my hair pure white overnight it did," croaked Jeffreys.

"What did she look like?" asked Dexter.

"Long pale hair, a floaty white dress and terrible eyes! I'll never forget those eyes of hers until the day I die!" quavered Jeffreys.

"Why?" said Dexter.

"They flashed on and off and glowed in the dark like hot coals!"

"Sounds scary!" said Dexter with a shiver. "Who was Lady Grizel?"

"She lived in the castle nearly three hundred years ago. There's an old portrait of her in the West Wing," said Jeffreys.

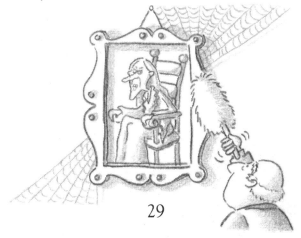

"No, there isn't!" snapped Uncle Igor. "It was a hideous-looking painting, so I've tucked it away in the attic. I'm thinking of selling it at the local car boot sale!"

Jeffreys looked nervously over his shoulder as if he was worried Lady Grizel would hear him. "Please be

careful what you say, sir. I've heard that Lady Grizel was famed for her bad temper. She's one of your ancestors, after all – bad tempers must run in the family."

"BAD TEMPERS DO NOT RUN IN THE FAMILY!" shouted Uncle Igor, bashing the table with his fist.

"Sorry, sir," croaked Jeffreys.

Uncle Igor calmed down. His eyes gleamed wickedly in the candlelight as a smile spread slowly across his face. "Tonight, Dexter my lad, you can film a real live ghost, eh! What?"

"But ghosts are dead, aren't they?" said Dexter.

"Oh no, not the ghost of Lady Grizel. She's very much alive and kicking," said Uncle Igor, and he gave Dexter a crafty wink.

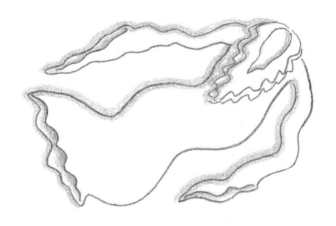

Chapter 3

The Floaty White Nightie

Uncle Igor took a gold watch on a chain from somewhere in his black velvet cloak. "It's eleven o'clock. We're going to have some fun tonight, eh! What?"

"Why did you get me up here?" panted Dexter. They were right at the top of the castle in the dusty attic.

It was as big as a football pitch.

"I'm going to dress up as the ghost of Lady Grizel and put the frighteners on old Jeffreys!" said Uncle Igor, his eyes sparkling. "And you're going to film the look on his face with your new video camera!"

"We wouldn't want to scare him too much," said Dexter.

"Don't be such a party pooper! He's going to take at least ten years to recover from the kind of shock I'm going to give him! Check no one has followed us up here."

Dexter glanced around the attic.

It was full of crumbly wooden boxes with old hats and shoes flopping out.

A painting of a woman in an old-fashioned dress was propped up in a corner. For a second Dexter thought he saw one of her eyes wink.

"No one has followed us up here, but it's giving me the creeps. I feel as if we're being watched," said Dexter.

"You're letting your imagination run away with you, young fellow. Do you know who that is?" said Uncle Igor, jabbing a bony finger in the direction of the painting.

"Lady Grizel?" guessed Dexter.

"That's her all right. Looked spooky enough when she was still alive, judging by the look of that painting! Ugly old bag, eh! What?"

"And will she really stalk the castle at midnight?" asked Dexter.

"What? Oh – that old story. I've never seen her. But tonight – she'll walk again! Now close your eyes and don't open them until I tell you."

Dexter squeezed his eyes shut.

"You can open them now," said Uncle Igor.

Dexter opened his eyes, but for a minute he thought they were still closed. Uncle Igor had switched off the light and the attic was pitch black.

"Yoo hoo! I'm over here. Can you see me?" called Uncle Igor.

Dexter peered into the darkness. "I can see something tall and white."

"It's me! Do I look like Lady Grizel, the spooky old bag?"

"It's hard to tell, I can't see you that well."

"I'll switch the light back on," said Uncle Igor.

Dexter nearly burst out laughing. Uncle Igor stood in front of him wearing a floaty white nightie. A lacy white tablecloth hung down over his face, held in place by a ring of plastic daisies.

"How do I look? Good, eh! What?" said Uncle Igor proudly.

"Something's not quite right. I think it's the eyes. Jeffreys said they flashed on and off and glowed in the dark like hot coals," said Dexter.

41

"Ah yes, the eyes! I'm not known as a genius for nothing! I've made a little contraption. . ." said Uncle Igor, taking a rubber ring from a pocket in his nightie.

It was the type of ring you buy in a pet shop for a dog to play with. Uncle Igor carefully placed the rubber ring on top of his head. "Must watch the old daisies, eh! What?" he said and carefully pulled the ring down over his forehead until it was just above his eyes.

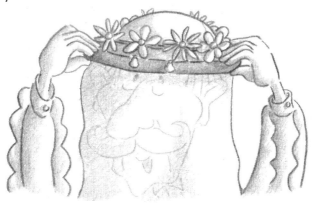

"What are you doing, Uncle?" said Dexter.

"I'm about to show you my brilliant invention," said Uncle Igor.

At the front of the rubber ring were two small light-bulbs. From one side of the ring trailed a wire, and at the end of the wire dangled a rubber ball.

"Turn off the light again," ordered Uncle Igor.

Dexter switched off the light.

"Ooooh! Whooo! Ooooh! Whooo! Will I make old Jeffreys turn to jelly in his Dr Martens? Are you shivering? Are you quivering? Are you shaking in your shoes?" groaned Uncle Igor as he shuffled towards Dexter, his light-bulb eyes flashing on, off, on, off.

"I'm goose-pimply all over!" lied Dexter. "How do you make the eyes flash on and off like that?"

"Simple, dear fellow. I squeeze this rubber ball and . . . hey presto! The eyes light up. Good stuff, eh! What?"

Chapter 4

The Ghost of Lady Grizel

It was ten to midnight. Uncle Igor and Dexter were in the castle's banqueting hall. Threadbare tapestries shivered in the breeze, and bats flitted above their heads like tatty black dishcloths.

"What we'll do. . ." whispered Uncle Igor, peering around the banqueting hall and ducking as a bat swooped over, "is this. We'll hide behind these suits of armour, and I'll jump out at Jeffreys at the stroke of midnight."

"How do you know Jeffreys will come into the banqueting hall at midnight? He might be in bed snoring by then," said Dexter.

"Oh, no! Not Jeffreys! The old fellow troops around the castle from eleven-forty-five until twelve-thirty, locking everything up for the night. He'll reach the banqueting hall at midnight."

"He works long hours if he's still about at midnight. He has to get up at five in the morning to start cooking your breakfast – I bet he's exhausted by the end of the day," said Dexter.

"Rubbish! Hard work never hurt

anyone!" snapped Uncle Igor.

A flash of lightning blazed through the stained-glass windows and lit up the banqueting hall in rainbow colours, while thunder rumbled and grumbled across the sky outside.

"As soon as you see me jump out – start filming," said Uncle Igor.

"Yes, Uncle," said Dexter.

"Good show! Thirty seconds to go and counting."

Dexter heard the sound of heavy footsteps. The footsteps clomped nearer, nearer, nearer.

"He's coming!" said Dexter in a loud whisper.

"Sssssh!" hissed Uncle Igor.

The footsteps echoed around the stone walls and bounced off the flagstones. Dexter poked his head out from behind the suit of armour, his video camera to his eye. Uncle Igor strode majestically into the middle of the hall. The long white nightie floated out behind him, and the light-bulb eyes flashed on, off, on, off.

The footsteps stopped outside the door. The door gave a groan. Slowly, slowly, slowly, it creaked open. A woman plodded into the room. She had long pale hair, and her face was hidden by a veil held in place by a ring of weeds and old dandelions.

"HELP!" shouted Uncle Igor, taking a flying leap behind a suit of armour. There was a loud ripping sound as he put his foot through his long white nightie. "IT'S LADY GRIZEL!" he screeched at the top of his voice. "THE REAL GHOST! CRIPES! SAVE ME!"

Uncle Igor grabbed Dexter and held him in front of him.

The ghost of Lady Grizel plodded around the hall then stalked slowly towards them.

"What's it doing? Make it go away!" shouted Uncle Igor.

Lady Grizel paused in front of the rows of armour. "I have a message. Come out from behind that suit of armour," she said in a low, spooky voice.

Uncle Igor pushed Dexter forward.

"Erm. . ." Dexter began, wondering what to say to a ghost.

"My message is for Igor and none other than Igor," said Lady Grizel impatiently.

Uncle Igor peeped out. "Coo-eee! I'm here! At your service, dear lady!"

"My message concerns your faithful butler, Jeffreys," said Lady Grizel.

"Jeffreys?" said Uncle Igor.

"You have a hundred spare bedrooms in your castle and yet he sleeps in the dungeon. Is that correct?"

"Yes, Your Ladyship, but it's very comfy down there," lied Uncle Igor.

"Did you offer to buy him a new cat after Hector met with that unfortunate accident?" said Lady Grizel.

"Well, you see, it was like this —" began Uncle Igor.

"Did you offer him a clean hanky to mop up his tears?"

"W–w–we don't do our laundry until a week on Tuesday," stuttered Uncle Igor.

"How much do you pay Jeffreys? I expect Dexter gets more pocket money in a week than you pay Jeffreys in a year!"

Uncle Igor hung his head.

"Find him a new cat, pay him fairly and he's to work no more than three hours per day. Is that clear?"

"Yes, dear lady," said Uncle Igor, bowing and wringing his hands together at the same time. "Anything you say, eh! What?"

"I've not finished with you yet!" commanded Lady Grizel as Uncle Igor scuttled back behind a suit of armour. "You're to move Jeffreys into the master bedroom – the one with the cosy fireplace and the four-poster bed with the feather pillows."

"Look here, Lady Grizel," spluttered Uncle Igor. "That's *my* room!"

Lady Grizel came closer. She reached out towards Uncle Igor with a stringy arm. Her eyes flashed.

"I'll move out tomorrow," said Uncle Igor hastily.

Lady Grizel curtseyed. "Very well, but mark my words. If you don't do as I say I'll haunt your castle night and day for the next five hundred years!"

"I promise, Your Ladyship. Anything, anything at all!" gasped Uncle Igor, staggering backwards.

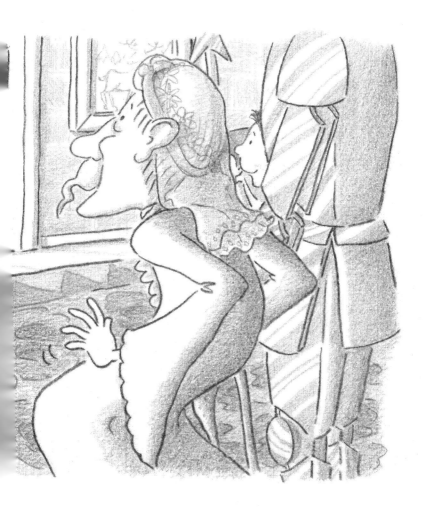

The ghost of Lady Grizel stalked back towards the door. "Farewell! Keep your promise," she said, and waved a pale, limp hand as she left the room.

"Jeepers! Did you capture that on film?" said Uncle Igor.

"Yeah! Wasn't it great?" said Dexter.

"A real, live ghost! Well I never! Eh! What?"

Chapter 5

Jeffreys

The next day Dexter shoved a tangle of jeans, jumpers and trainers back into his suitcase then raced downstairs.

"Enjoyed your stay?" said Uncle Igor.

"Fantastic!" panted Dexter.

"You've got your film to watch when you get back."

"I'll put the video in as soon as I get home," said Dexter.

"Hope you can find some kind of explanation as to why I'm wearing a floaty white nightie in it. Wouldn't want your mum to think I'd lost my marbles, eh! What?"

"Don't worry, Uncle Igor. I'll say you're wearing the nightie because you find pyjamas uncomfy," said Dexter.

"Good thinking! Where's your suitcase?"

"I've left it upstairs," groaned Dexter.

At that moment Jeffreys plodded down the sweeping stone staircase, carrying Dexter's suitcase.

"Nobody saw you carrying that down, did they?" said Uncle Igor, turning pale.

"No, sir," croaked Jeffreys.

"You look as if you could do with a nap, Jeffreys," said Uncle Igor. "Come with me – I've got a surprise for you."

Uncle Igor took Jeffreys' arm and led him back up the stone staircase. Dexter followed close behind.

"I'm not in trouble, am I, sir?" whimpered Jeffreys.

"Nothing of the sort!" said Uncle Igor as they arrived at the top of the stairs. He threw open a door and cried, "TA DA!"

Jeffreys and Dexter looked into a cosy bedroom. A big fire crackled in the hearth, the feather pillows were plumped up on the four-poster bed and a pot of tea was placed on a china tray with a plate of chocolate biscuits.

"For you, Jeffreys," said Uncle Igor. "A new bedroom, eh! What?"

"Thank you, sir," croaked Jeffreys.

"That's not all. . ." said Uncle Igor, winking at Dexter. "Look under the bed."

Jeffreys' knees cracked as he peered underneath the bed. A moment later

he popped up again with a tiny ginger kitten wriggling in his arms.

"I paid a visit to the animal sanctuary this morning," said Uncle Igor.

"Oh, sir, he's beautiful!" gasped Jeffreys.

"Dexter and I will leave you alone with him to make friends," said Uncle Igor, closing the door.

"That was great! I never thought you'd do what Lady Grizel told you!" said Dexter.

Uncle Igor peered around nervously. "Marvellous woman," he muttered.

"Must get her portrait back up in the West Wing, eh! What?"

Chapter 6

The Movie

After a long train journey, Dexter arrived home. Dexter and his mum settled down on the settee in front of the television.

"I'm looking forward to seeing this video of yours. Uncle Igor's always up to something," said Mum.

"Wait until you see this!" said Dexter.

The TV screen flickered. Uncle Igor appeared – a ghostly, shadowy figure in white.

"What on earth is he wearing?" said Mum.

"It's a nightie – he finds pyjamas uncomfy," said Dexter hastily.

Suddenly Uncle Igor charged towards the camera, his face as white as his nightie, his eyes popping like a couple of footballs about to burst.

"What's the matter with him? He looks as if he's seen a ghost," said Mum.

"He has," said Dexter as the figure of Lady Grizel came on to the screen.

"Who's that?" said Mum.

"It's the ghost of Lady Grizel.'

"It's the first ghost I've seen that wears Dr Martens boots!" said Mum with a laugh.

Dexter peered at the screen. Sure enough, poking out from the hem of Lady Grizel's dress was a pair of Dr Martens boots.

"It's Jeffreys!" said Dexter, giggling.

"And who is that?" said Mum, pointing at the screen. "I didn't know anybody else was staying at the castle."

Dexter peered again at the TV screen. Standing behind Jeffreys was a tall lady wearing a long floaty dress. Her eyes glowed like hot coals as they flashed on, off, on, off.

"That really *is* Lady Grizel!" gasped Dexter.

"Poor Uncle Igor. . .!"

The End

Bumps in the Night

FRANK RODGERS

Illustrated by Philip Hopman

Chapter 1

Sam and Katie Pickle were excited.

Their mum and dad had bought a little café in a country village and the family were going to live in the flat above it. The café was called The Hungry Horse and the Pickles were thrilled to bits with it.

"It looks so cosy and welcoming," smiled Mr Pickle.

"It's going to be the best café in the world," replied Mrs Pickle, and Sam and Katie agreed.

On the day of their arrival they went to buy food at the village store. It was then that people began to talk.

"You've bought The Hungry Horse Café?" gasped Mrs Kettle in surprise, her hairy eyebrows doing a little dance. "But it's haunted, you know."

"Yes, indeed," agreed Mr Faucett, the greengrocer, "by a thing that goes bump in the night."

"And what a noise it makes too!" cried little Miss Mantle. "*Bump . . . ooooh! Bump . . . ooooh!*"

"Very scary," they all said.
"Oh, dear," said Mr Pickle.

"Not only that," Miss Mantle went on, her little eyes jumping up and down like ping-pong balls, "but it's probably the ghost of a rascally robber or a horrible hairy highwayman. So many things have gone missing in the village over the years, you see."

"They certainly have," Mrs Chimmly chimed in. "That café of yours should be called The Greedy Ghost!"

"What sort of things have gone missing?" asked Mrs Pickle.

"My silver watch and chain," said Mr Faucett.

"My gold ring," said Mrs Kettle.

"My brass thimble," said Mrs Chimmly.

"My little cut-glass perfume bottle," said Miss Mantle.

"Lots of other things too," said Mr Faucett. "And we're sure that the ghost is responsible."

"Oh, dear," said Mr Pickle.

Chapter 2

That night, as she and Sam settled down to sleep in the little flat above the café, Katie said, "Do you really think there is a ghost, Mum?"

Mrs Pickle laughed. "I wouldn't think so, Katie," she said. "People sometimes let their imaginations run away with them. I don't think it's a ghost who is stealing those things from the people in the village, do you?"

Katie shook her head slowly. "No. . ." she replied.

Then Sam piped up. "But what causes the bumps in the night, Mum?"

"Oh, the bumps in the night are probably caused by the old plumbing, Sam. Air in the pipes makes them bang," she said.

"Or it could be the timbers of the house creaking and groaning like old bones," said his dad. "This is an old building. Old buildings complain, you know."

They kissed Sam and Katie goodnight and went to bed themselves.

"Bumps in the night," scoffed Katie when they were left alone. "*Bump . . . ooooh . . . bump . . . ooooh. . .* Of course it's just the plumbing!"

"Yes," agreed Sam. "Just the old house complaining."

"Or," giggled Katie, "it could be an elephant clog-dancing on the roof *Bump . . . ta-raaa! Bump . . . ta-raaa!*"

Sam laughed and joined in the fun. "Or a gorilla on a pogo stick. *Bump . . . wheee! Bump . . . wheee!*"

They were both laughing now.

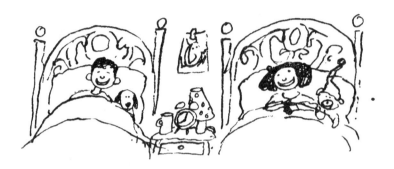

"It could be a pirate with a wooden leg!" cried Katie. "*Bump . . . ooo-aar! Bump . . . ooo-aar!*"

Their bubbling laughter rang round the room. It filled up their ears so much that at first they didn't hear the noises.

Then Katie suddenly said, "Shhh! Listen, Sam!"

Sam stopped laughing and listened.

Faintly, from above their heads in the attic, came some unmistakable sounds.

Bump . . . ooooh! Bump . . . ooooh!

"Oh!" gasped Sam. "Katie . . . you don't think. . .?"

Bump . . . ooooh! went the noises, a little louder this time.

"It's just the plumbing!" squeaked Katie.

Bump . . . ooooh. . .!

"Or the old timbers!" squealed Sam, jumping on to his sister's bed.

BUMP . . . OOOH!

"Aaah!" they gasped. "It's the ghost! The house is haunted after all!" And they rushed out of their bedroom and into Mum and Dad's.

The Pickles huddled together on the big bed and listened.

BUMP . . . OOOOH! BUMP . . . OOOOH!

"Er . . . it's just the plumbing," said Mr Pickle.

"Or the old timbers. . ." said Mrs Pickle.

BUMP . . . OOOOH . . . OOOOH!

"Are you sure?" asked Sam and Katie.

"Well . . . perhaps it would be a good idea if we made up beds for you in our room for tonight," said Mum and Dad.

Chapter 3

Next morning in the bright sunshine the little flat above the café didn't seem scary at all.

"We were very silly yesterday," said Mr Pickle. "Imagine being scared of a few bumps in the night."

"Why don't we look around?" suggested Mrs Pickle. "We might find out what's causing the noises."

"Yes!" cried Sam and Katie. "Let's explore!"

So they searched every nook and cranny, poking their noses into corners and cupboards. Mr Pickle checked the piping and tapped on the walls. He even looked up the chimney.

But nowhere did they find anything that might have made the *bump* . . . *oooh!* noises.

"What about the attic?" said Katie.

"Oh, dear, I'd forgotten all about that," said Mr Pickle.

He got the ladder out and propped it up against the hatch.

Up he went.

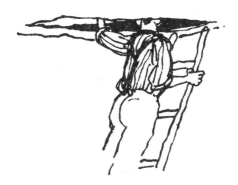

Creeeak. . . The wooden hatch groaned as Mr Pickle pushed it open. The rest of the family gazed up at him and held their breath.

"What do you see?" asked Mrs Pickle.

"Well. . ." said Mr Pickle, "there's a lot of old furniture lying around."

"Can we come up and look?" asked Sam.

"I don't see why not," answered his dad. "It seems perfectly safe."

One by one they climbed the ladder and went into the attic.

It was like the inside of a junk shop. Chairs and tables, trunks and boxes, drawers and cupboards lying higgledy-piggledy. There was even an old rocking-horse.

"It's wonderful!" cried Sam.

"Like Aladdin's Cave!" exclaimed Katie.

Mr Pickle pointed to a hole in the roof. "Look," he said, "that could explain all the noises. The wind could whistle through that gap. . ."

"Going *ooooh*. . ." smiled Mrs Pickle.

"Yes," grinned Mr Pickle, "and it could move the rocking-horse, making it go *bump*!"

"So there you are," said Mrs Pickle smugly. "It's all explained. There is no ghost."

Katie leaned close to Sam and whispered, "I was hoping we really had a ghost, Sam."

Sam nodded and whispered back, "Me too. It would've been fun."

The Pickles then began to explore the attic and Katie opened a little trunk and looked inside.

"Oh, look everyone!" she said. "Old photographs."

She picked them up and handed them round.

"Here's one of The Hungry Horse Café," said Mr Pickle.

Mrs Pickle looked at the faded black and white photograph and said, "My goodness, this must have been taken a long, long time ago."

"Who's that old man standing in front of the café?" asked Sam.

His mum turned the photograph over and saw there was some faint writing on the back.

"As far as I can make out it says *T. Greenberry. Proprietor*," she said. "He must have been the original owner."

"This photograph would look lovely hanging in our café," said Mr Pickle. "It would be a nice link with the past."

Katie looked at the old man again. "He looks nice," she said.

Sam nodded in agreement. "Smiley," he said. "As if he really loved living here."

"Maybe he still does," Katie whispered to Sam, taking him aside.

"You mean. . ." Sam began.

"Yes," whispered Katie, her eyes sparkling. "I think we've found our ghost!"

Chapter 4

That night, Katie and Sam lay awake, waiting.

The minutes ticked by towards midnight and they became sleepier and sleepier.

"Perhaps there isn't a ghost after all," murmured Sam.

Katie yawned and snuggled down,

sighing. "Perhaps you're right," she said.

Bump . . . ooooh!

Katie and Sam sat bolt upright in their beds. "What was that?" they cried.

Bump . . . ooooh! went the noise again.

Their bedroom door opened and in came Mum and Dad.

"It's the ghost!" chorused Katie and Sam.

Mr Pickle shook his head. "It's just the wind blowing through that hole in the roof," he said. "Go back to sleep."

But Katie and Sam got out of bed.

"I think we should go and look," said Katie.

Mum glanced at Dad and they both shrugged.

"Why not?" said Mrs Pickle. "Let's find out once and for all."

Bump . . . ooooh!

Everyone looked up.

"The noise is definitely coming from the attic," said Mr Pickle. "Let's investigate."

Once more he put the ladder up against the hatch. "Er . . . it'll probably be dark up there," he said, unsure.

"Perhaps I should fetch a torch?"

"We don't have one, dear," said Mrs Pickle, and before Mr Pickle could protest, she began to climb the ladder.

Stealthily she crept upwards.

Creeeaak . . . The hatch opened and she disappeared into the attic.

A few seconds later Mrs Pickle poked her head down through the opening and whispered, "Come on up."

One by one they followed her until all four were standing together among the shadowy bits of furniture. The moonlight shone in through the small window and the hole in the roof, and the light in the hall shone up from below so the attic wasn't as dark as Mr Pickle had feared.

Sam looked at the rocking-horse and gasped. "Oh!" he cried. "Look . . . it's moving!

Mr Pickle smiled. "Ah," he said, "just as I thought. The wind has blown in through the hole and —"

Bump . . . OOOOH!

Everyone jumped.

The noise had come from behind them!

Startled, everyone whirled round and saw. . .

The ghost!

It was the kindly old man from the photograph.

"I knew it!" Katie whispered in glee and Sam grinned from ear to ear.

The old man didn't seem to have noticed them. He stood beside a small table rubbing his shin and shaking his head. "Can't see a thing without my glasses," he muttered. "Keep on bumping into things."

Mr and Mrs Pickle gaped at him in astonishment.

"Oh, dear," murmured Mr Pickle. "I was wrong. We *do* have a ghost."

"This house is haunted after all," gasped Mrs Pickle.

"Hooray!" yelled Sam and Katie.

"What . . . who?" The ghost looked up sharply and bumped his head on a brass lampshade. *Bump!* "Ooooh!" he cried.

He rubbed his head and stared at the family. "Who are you?" he asked.

"Er . . . we're the Pickle family," replied Mr Pickle. "We live here now."

"Ah," said the ghost, "of course . . . the new owners." He bowed.

"Delighted to meet you. My name is Tobias Greenberry. I built this place, you know, and lived here up to my death a hundred years ago." He smiled. "I liked it so much I couldn't bear to leave it. That's why I'm still here."

"You're the thing that goes bump in the night!" cried Katie.

Tobias nodded ruefully and rubbed his head and then his shin. "I've lost my glasses, you see. Can't see properly without them. Keep on bumping into things."

"And going *ooooh!*" said Sam with a grin.

Tobias nodded again. "Sorry if I disturbed you," he said. "It's just that some ghosts are more solid than others. That's why I bump into things rather than go *through* them." He rubbed his shin again. "You haven't come across a pair of glasses, have you?"

The Pickles shook their heads.

"I'm afraid not," said Mr Pickle.

The old man sighed. "Looks like I'll just have to blunder around going *bump . . . ooooh* until I find them," he said.

"Perhaps someone took them," suggested Katie.

"Yes," said Sam, "the same person who took the things from the people in the village."

"Oh," said Tobias. "You mean other things have gone missing as well?"

Mrs Pickle nodded. "The people in the village think that you're to blame, Tobias. They said that the café should be called The Greedy Ghost."

Tobias was shocked. "What?" he cried. "But that's terrible! I've never stolen anything in my life. How can people think that of me? I must clear my name . . . but how?"

As the family pondered on this the moon came out from behind a cloud and bathed everything in a silvery glow.

Suddenly something caught Sam's eye.

"Look," he said, stepping forward and picking up a large black feather and two small grey ones. "Where did these come from?"

Mr Pickle examined them and nodded his head.

"Aha!" he said with a grin. "I think we may have found our robber!"

Mrs Pickle looked at the feathers and smiled too. "These are a jackdaw's feathers," she said.

"Yes . . . they like to take things, don't they?" said Katie.

"Bright, shiny things," said Sam.

"Like thimbles, rings, watches. . ." said Mr Pickle.

"And glasses!" cried Tobias. He clapped his hands. "Come to think of it, I have seen a jackdaw coming and going through that hole in the roof. Do you really think that it could be to blame for all the missing things?"

"It certainly could," said Mr Pickle. "And we're going to find out, Tobias . . . tomorrow!"

Chapter 5

After breakfast next morning the Pickle family went into the back garden. Tobias's pale face peered at them from the attic window, watching anxiously.

There were quite a few trees in the garden and also quite a few birds flying about. Amid the whistling and trilling of the birds the Pickles heard loud, harsh, *tchack* . . . *tchack* sounds.

"That," said Mr Pickle, "is our friend the jackdaw."

They heard them again and Katie pointed. "There!" she cried.

Everyone looked up into the huge chestnut tree at the bottom of the garden. Just visible near the top was the dark shape of a large nest. Out of it flew a black bird with a grey band round the lower part of its head.

"That's the jackdaw, all right," exclaimed Mr Pickle.

He went into the outhouse and returned with a long ladder which he propped against the tree.

"Be careful, dear," called Mrs Pickle as he began to climb.

"I will," replied Mr Pickle, as he went higher and higher.

The jackdaw was annoyed at the intrusion and flapped around the tree, croaking loudly like a stick rattling against a fence.

A few seconds later, Mr Pickle disappeared from sight into the foliage of the tree. The family waited anxiously below for him to reappear again.

Tobias hadn't moved from the window in the attic.

Minutes passed and Mr Pickle didn't appear.

"Oh, dear," said Mrs Pickle. "I do hope he's all right."

Just then Mr Pickle's legs came into view as he climbed back down the ladder.

"Hooray!" shouted Sam and Katie. "Dad's okay!"

In the attic Tobias jumped for joy and bumped his head against the brass lamp again.

Bump! "Ooooh!"

Mr Pickle descended slowly towards his wife and children. When he reached the ground they saw that he was smiling happily.

"It was like a blooming treasure trove up there!" he said, laughing.

"That jackdaw's nest was stuffed with all sorts of bright things." He reached into the big pockets of his jacket and brought out things which glittered in the sunlight.

A brass thimble . . . a silver watch and chain . . . a cut-glass perfume bottle . . . a gold ring . . . a diamond brooch . . . a silver spoon . . . and finally, a pair of glasses.

He held the things up one by one to show Tobias. The pale, ghostly face at the window peered hard, then broke into a huge grin. It disappeared from view as Tobias jumped for joy again.

Down from the attic drifted the familiar *bump . . . ooooh!*

The family laughed.

"Poor Tobias," said Mrs Pickle. "But I'm sure that's the last time he'll bump into anything now he's got his glasses back."

"And he'll be delighted that his name is cleared at last," said Mr Pickle. "We must give these things back and tell everyone who the *real* robber was!"

Chapter 6

Tobias was thrilled to bits. He danced round and round the attic laughing and singing happily. And because he was wearing his glasses he didn't bump into one thing.

"It'll be nice and quiet up here from now on, won't it, Tobias," grinned Mr Pickle.

"It certainly will," replied Tobias, "because now that I've found my glasses I can wander about all over the house."

"Oh. . ." said Mr Pickle. "*All* over the house, Tobias? Including the café?"

"Especially the café!" replied Tobias cheerfully. "Oh, it'll be so nice to go back to my old haunts again!"

"But. . ." stammered Mr Pickle, "won't you frighten away our customers?"

"Oh, don't worry about that," smiled Tobias. "I'll stay in the kitchen until they get used to me. I used to be a great cook, you know. In fact," he added happily, "since I've become a ghost I've learnt some terrific new recipes!"

"Fantastic!" cried Sam and Katie. "We'll have a spook for a cook!"

Everyone roared with laughter.

And that is why The Hungry Horse Café was renamed The Spooky Cook Café and became famous throughout the countryside for some rather strange dishes on its menu. . .

Ghosted Cheese. . .

Spook-etti. . .

I-Scream. . .

And a yummy cake covered in black icing, silver stars and big lumps of dark chocolate called *Bumps In The Night*.

The End

Scarem's House

MALCOLM YORKE

Illustrated by Terry McKenna

Chapter 1

At the end of a humpy, bumpy track deep in the countryside there was a gloomy wood. In the middle of this wood stood a derelict house which nobody had lived in, or even visited, for many years. The house was not empty, though – it was inhabited by a family of ghosts.

There was a father ghost called Scarem

O'Gool, his wife Panic O'Gool and their twins, Gob and Lin O'Gool. Their ghost dog, Dreary, lived in a mouldy cupboard in what had once been the kitchen, and a ghost owl, called Howl, had his perch on a dusty beam in the attic.

As everyone knows, all ghosts sleep through the day because they don't like sunshine. The wood was so gloomy and the windows so dirty and cobwebby that very little light could get into the house, which made it splendidly damp and chilly for them.

All the O'Gools slept on rotten leaves on the floor. Scarem and Panic had the big bedroom, where part of the ceiling had fallen down. Gob and Lin had a smaller room, where fungus grew on the walls and toadstools came out of the spongy floorboards.

They all thought the house was lovely and creepy, and in that droopy, dismal kind of way that ghost families have, the O'Gools were quite content.

Every evening when the sun had set, they would get up and have breakfast in the dark. Of course ghosts cannot eat solid food, instead, they feed by smelling things. Favourites are a good waft of stagnant water, a sniff of mildew, the scent of mould and a pinch of rust. There were plenty of these delicious ghost foods scattered around their crumbling house.

After breakfast Gob and Lin always took Dreary for his midnight walk in the wood, where he would chase ghost rabbits and bark mournfully. At the same time Howl would glide off to hunt ghost mice in the undergrowth. For the rest of the night the family would flit around, giving the odd groan or *whoooooooo*! until the sun rose and it was time to go back to their mouldy beds.

Sometimes, as a special treat, they would all shimmer off to the churchyard five miles away, where they would spend a satisfyingly miserable hour or two moaning and wailing round the graves. On their way back through the village they might make a half-hearted effort to rattle a few doorknobs or howl down a chimney and tap on a window. Nobody in the village ever seemed to notice these things, but the O'Gools weren't bothered because they didn't want to have any close contact with humans. People were all far too cheery and noisy for the timid ghosts.

It was a very lonely, very boring and very joyless life, and they had lived like this for two hundred and fifty years.

Chapter 2

One sunny day, the O'Gools were woken up by a creak-creak-creaking from the front door. What could it be? The twins ran straight through the wall into their parents' room and clung to them as the door creaked again. Then it slammed open! They all jumped in terror. Dreary shot up the stairs yelping with fright and Howl fluttered down through the ceiling to see what was wrong. Next they heard footsteps – human footsteps on the floorboards below. Then – horror of horrors – human voices! How the O'Gools shivered and shook.

"Of course the house needs a few things doing to it, Mr Merry," said a man's voice.

"Oh, I can see that all right!" replied another man's voice with a great booming laugh.

"Perhaps we should knock it down and start again," said a jolly woman's voice.

"I admit it's in need of repair, but of course that's why the price is so low," came the first voice again.

More doors banged and footsteps pounded downstairs, then a boy yelled, "Wow! Come and look at this cellar Joy – it's really creepy!"

"Yeah! Spooky!" a girl replied. "Race you up the stairs!" And they thundered up in spite of shouts from the house agent to watch out for the rotten steps and bannisters.

The rest of the humans came upstairs too and began to explore every room. The ghosts, remembering that humans could not see or hear them, followed, still quivering with fright.

"And we could always grow our own mushrooms in here!" observed Mrs Merry with a laugh, putting her hand on the slimy plaster in Gob and Lin's room.

"True, but try to picture the rooms with nice cheerful wallpaper and a coat of paint," pleaded the young man.

"There's plenty of fresh air, I see," chuckled Mr Merry, pointing to a huge hole in the roof. He was short and energetic-looking and had curly red hair.

"Well, yes, but a few tiles would soon put that right," said the young man, who was trying his best to sell this awful old ruin.

Meanwhile, the two children were exploring and yelling to each other.

"Cor! Gregory, come and have a sniff in this cupboard!"

"Whew! What a pong! And now come and look up this chimney – I can see the sky!"

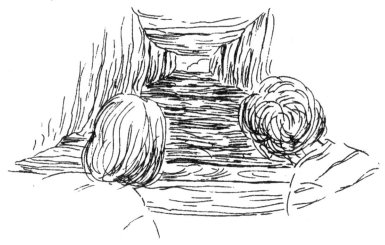

The ghosts followed the humans back down the stairs into the kitchen, getting more and more worried with every step. Were these horrible cheery people going to come and live in their home?

"Oh, this is far too dark to cook in. We'd need to put a big window in there and knock that wall through," said Mrs Merry, pointing.

"Maybe you're right, madam, but I can recommend a good local builder who could do that with no trouble at all," the salesman said.

The tour continued through the other rotting old rooms, the children running ahead and jumping up and down on the floorboards.

"Careful, you two, or you'll drop through into the cellar where all the ghosties are!" chortled Mr Merry and everybody laughed.

"Now, sir and madam, what do you think of it?" asked the salesman when they had seen everything.

"Well," said Mr Merry. "It's certainly a challenge. It would take a lot of money and a lot of paint, wallpaper, carpets, lights, plumbing, electricity and gardening to put it right."

"And we'd need a good road and a drive to the front door so we could get the car and the furniture van here," Mrs Merry pointed out. But there was a gleam in her eye as if she would enjoy all the bustle and planning.

"And then of course the milkman could deliver our milk and the postman could bring us letters and birthday cards and all our friends could drive up and we'd have barbecues and parties," added Mr Merry.

"So will you take it?" asked the salesman hopefully.

"I think we will," Mr and Mrs Merry said together.

"Great!" yelled the children so loudly that more plaster came tumbling down from the ceiling.

"I'm so glad," said the salesman, obviously relieved to be rid of the damp old dump.

"And I think even Felicity our cat will enjoy it here with the woods to hunt mice and rabbits in," said Mr Merry as he shook hands with the salesman on the deal.

Chapter 3

The Merry family went out, slamming the old door shut behind them, and the ghostly O'Gools were left in a state of shock.

Scarem was also furious. "My father built this house and now these humans are just going to sell it over our heads! It's already occupied! By us! Don't ghosts have any rights at all?"

"Did you hear what they said?" wailed Panic. "Paint! Wallpaper! Carpets! Ugh! I've kept this as a nice depressing house all these two hundred and fifty miserable years and now they're going to come in and spoil it all."

"Electricity!" snorted Scarem in disgust. "That means lights and radiators and those new-fangled television things we've seen in the village. Sheer vandalism!"

"And doesn't plumbing mean there'll be nasty hot water?" asked Gob.

"And what does a party mean? And what's a barbecue?" enquired Lin.

"Two revolting human children about the place laughing and playing and enjoying themselves all day – we'll never get to sleep!" Panic declared indignantly.

Dreary moaned and Howl hooted dolefully as they thought about Felicity the cat and all the troubles *she* would cause.

The ghosts were now even more miserable than usual, but this time they were not enjoying it. They sulked and drooped around the house gloomily waiting to see what would happen next.

Chapter 4

A few days later the O'Gools heard voices and the sound of machinery nearby. When they went to look after dark they found work had begun on turning the humpy bumpy lane into a smooth road leading to the garden gate. A week later they were woken by the arrival of a car. The invasion of their home had begun.

"Well, here we are, folks! Welcome to Merry Mansion!" boomed Mr Merry as he threw all the doors and windows wide open to let the sunshine in. The ghosts gibbered in fear.

There were bangs and clatters and yells all morning and at midday Mrs Merry used a little portable stove to heat some tomato soup and pies for lunch. The sickening smell of warm food drifted through the house, making the ghosts rush outside holding their stomachs and noses. They fled to a cave in the woods and stayed there until dark.

When it was quiet enough to go back to the house, they found that Mr and Mrs Merry had repaired the roof and swept out all the rotten leaves they used as beds. All the cobwebs had gone and a fire had been lit in the fireplace. The warmth and smell of soap and disinfectant made their home seem absolutely disgusting.

Over the next few weeks the O'Gools got
very little sleep as Mr and Mrs Merry
replastered the walls and put up colourful
wallpaper. They replaced the rotten
woodwork and painted everything in dazzling
glossy colours. Next they put in a damp-proof
course, radiators, a washing-machine, cooker,
fridge, water heater and lights. Then came
carpets and a television. All day long Mr
Merry whistled as he worked and Mrs Merry
sang along with the music on her radio.

Outside the whole family helped cut the grass with an electric mower, planted flowers, trimmed the trees with a chain-saw, up-rooted brambles and made a huge bonfire of all the rubbish.

When the Merrys' furniture arrived the white fluffy cat, Felicity, came too. She immediately chose to sleep in a new cupboard in the kitchen corner where Dreary usually slept. The ghosts retreated to the attic. It was the only place left with a bit of dust and dark.

The O'Gools were horrified at the destruction of their house. No more draughts, no more damp, no more gloom, no more cobwebs – the place was shockingly warm, light, dry, clean and, worst of all, cheerful. They huddled together in the attic and whispered through the night. Whatever could they do to get rid of these awful humans and their dreadful laughter and jolly bustle? Something drastic had to be done! And quickly!

Chapter 5

On the evening the Merrys held their house-warming party Mr O'Gool called a family meeting.

"Somehow we've got to fight back," he declared, shaking his fist in the direction of the attic stairs. Sounds of dance music and whoops of laughter came drifting up from the party.

"Oh, this is terrible!" groaned Panic. "What'll we do, Scarem?"

"Hey, that's it, Panic!" Scarem exclaimed. "You've just given me an idea! That's what we'll do – we'll scare 'em."

"Good idea," said his wife. "After all, these humans are supposed to be frightened of us ghosts, aren't they?"

"And if we really scare them enough they'll leave, won't they?" said Gob.

"And take their disgusting wallpaper with them," added Lin.

"And their ghastly cat," muttered Dreary and Howl, who had both been badly frightened by Felicity's fierceness and the way she had taken over the wood as if she owned it.

The ghosts started to feel a bit more hopeful, especially when Scarem began to organize them.

"Now, if I remember what Grandfather O'Gool told me (and he lives in a haunted castle so he ought to know), what frightens these humans most is if you make sudden strange noises when they're not expecting them."

"And what about moving things around so they can't find them?" suggested Panic.

"Or we could let them get a glimpse of us in the distance, floating through walls and ceilings – that'll scare them," said Gob.

"They'll soon wish they'd never come!" Lin concluded with gloomy glee.

They all had a little practice at making sudden weird noises, moving things, and popping out of the plaster before they set off to haunt the Merry family. The plan was that Mr and Mrs O'Gool would tackle the parents and Gob and Lin would frighten the children. Dreary and Howl would take care of Felicity the cat.

Downstairs the party was hotting up. People were doing Highland reels in the sitting room so that when Scarem howled, "Whoooooooooooooooooooooooooooooooooo!" it wasn't even heard.

Mrs Merry's friends were chatting to her in the kitchen while she prepared the food. Panic tried moving the knives and forks and jellies and sandwiches and drinks around to confuse them, but they were talking so hard and in such a muddle already they never even noticed.

In the hall the children were having a race to see who could pop the most balloons by sitting on them, so that when Gob and Lin banged all the doors shut to scare them nobody took the slightest notice. They all tried and tried but not one of the humans was in the least bit bothered.

At last the party was over and the guests departed. Mr and Mrs Merry flopped into armchairs to watch the late night movie on television. Panic and Scarem thought this was a good chance to show themselves. They tried waving their arms about to get noticed, and even joined hands and danced in front of the television screen.

"Reception's not very good tonight, is it dear?" said Mr Merry.

"No, too many wavy lines," agreed Mrs Merry. "Give the telly a good thump!"

Meanwhile, upstairs Gob and Lin had found the children sitting up in their beds reading books. Both were wearing headphones and listening to music tapes at the same time.

"Yaaaaaaaaaaaaaaaaaaaaaa!" shrieked Gob.

"Booooooooooooooooooooo!" howled Lin.

Neither Joy nor Gregory looked up from their books – their earphones blocked out all other sounds.

Next Gob and Lin threw some books and toys on the floor and then some of the children's clothes, but the room was already so untidy with books, toys and clothes scattered all over the carpet, that neither of the children noticed.

Down in the kitchen Felicity was asleep in her cupboard. Dreary and Howl woke her by pulling her whiskers, which made her furious.

She couldn't see them, but she puffed up her fur and spat with such rage that Dreary and Howl fled back to the attic, badly scared. There they met the rest of the baffled ghosts.

"These humans are so noisy they can't even hear our howling," said Scarem in disgust.

"Those children will never notice if we move things around because their things don't have proper places anyway. The two of them are incredibly untidy!" complained Gob and Lin.

"And none of them can see us because all this awful light everywhere shines straight through us. So now what do we do?" asked Panic, scratching her head.

"I think I'll go over to Castle Dire and see Grandfather O'Gool and ask if we can borrow some real haunting equipment – you know, skulls and chains and white sheets and that kind of traditional spooky stuff," said Scarem. "I know they use them in the castle and they've scared a lot of people there."

The others agreed. It was obviously going to take some serious haunting to get rid of this stupid family of humans.

"This means war!" declared Scarem as he melted through the floor and set off to visit Grandfather O'Gool.

Chapter 6

The first time the O'Gools tried rattling chains outside the bedroom windows in the middle of the night, Mr Merry said, "Drat! I must have left the gate open," and got out of bed to close it.

"Funny, it was shut tight," he told Mrs Merry when he returned.

At first none of the humans seemed to

notice the ghosts floating around in white sheets, perhaps because the house was so bright they didn't show up. So Panic dyed them black and they tried again. After a few glimpses of floating black things going in and out of the walls Mrs Merry thought she needed spectacles and went to the optician's.

"It's strange, but he said my eyes were perfectly normal," she told Mr Merry.

Meanwhile, Gob and Lin were moving things around in the children's room.

"You've moved my radio from where I left it by my bed and put it in my pyjama drawer," Gregory accused Joy.

"No I never, and anyway, you've shifted my music tapes from my desk and dropped them in the wastepaper basket."

"That's not true and you know it!"

The children had a loud quarrel and after that they watched each other closely. Gob and Lin thought this was a good sign.

Down in the kitchen Felicity heard a dog barking and sharpened her claws ready to fight. She knew there were no dogs living within miles and this bark came from inside the house, so she searched and sniffed but found nothing, though she thought she saw a doggy tail whisk round the kitchen door.

Later there seemed to be an owl perched on a shelf, but when she leaped up to grab it all she did was bring the crockery tumbling and smashing down. Now Felicity was in disgrace with her humans, as well as being a very puzzled cat. Howl was very proud of this.

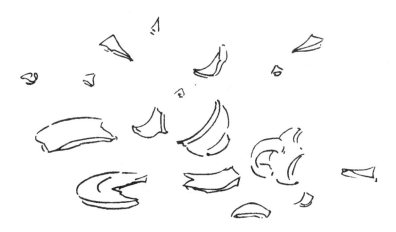

Mr Merry heard a long wailing coming down the chimney one night and thought it must be a strange kind of bird call. When he imitated it to a bird expert he was told there was no such thing. He was very baffled by this, especially as the next time he heard the wailing it came out of his wellington boot!

One day Mrs Merry thought she saw a human thigh bone in the vegetable rack, but when she picked it up it changed into a leek. "I really *do* need glasses," she muttered.

Once Gregory mistook his muddy football for a skull, and Joy could have sworn there was a shrunken head in the fruit bowl until she picked it up and found it was a shrivelled apple.

Mr Merry thought he glimpsed a hooded face peering over his shoulder as he was looking in the mirror to shave. He cut his chin.

One evening, the Merry family were playing a rowdy game of dominoes when they heard chains rattling upstairs. At the same time a radiator began to howl, whaaaaaa! and a hand holding a skull appeared through the wall above the fireplace and disappeared back again. A dog woofed in the kitchen and an owl hooted from the hallway, and all the doors in the house slammed shut, bang! bang! bang! one after the other. The Merrys sat up straight and looked very puzzled indeed.

"Now, that's very strange," said Mr Merry. "Just now I seemed to hear a lot of odd noises around the house – did anyone else hear them?"

"Yes, we did," they all agreed.

"And I've heard them before," added Mrs Merry.

"So have I," said Joy.

"And me," said Gregory.

Then they all recounted the peculiar things they had seen and heard over the past few days.

"I once saw a figure in a kind of black sheet follow me up the stairs," Mr Merry confessed.

"I heard an owl hoot in the bathroom, but there was no bird there and all the windows were shut," said Mrs Merry.

"I thought Joy had moved my secret diary, but it turned out that she didn't even know it existed," -said Gregory.

"And I thought he'd hidden all my pencils but then I found his pencils had been hidden too," said Joy.

"Well," concluded Mr Merry, "it looks to me as if there's only one explanation. We are sharing the house with ghosts!"

"Really? How very interesting!" said Mrs Merry. She was not in the least frightened.

"Wow! Great! Wait till we tell them at school!" exclaimed the children.

"Yes, this could be a lot of fun! Now, here's what we'll do, everybody," Mr Merry decided. "We'll all write down in this exercise book everything we hear and see from now on. Put the place and the time and the date as well, and at the end of a fortnight we'll see what kind of ghosts we've got. Agreed?"

Everyone agreed enthusiastically.

Chapter 7

Each day for the next two weeks, entries like these appeared in the book:

8·30 am Thursday.
Mrs M: Saw human skull in the breadbin. Disappeared when I put my hand in for loaf.
4·30pm Friday. Mr M:
Heard dog growling in toilet. Nothing there when I opened door.

10 pm Saturday.
Joy: Saw headless figure in
black sheet walking in corridor.
I waved and shouted hello but
it only walked up the wall and
through the ceiling.

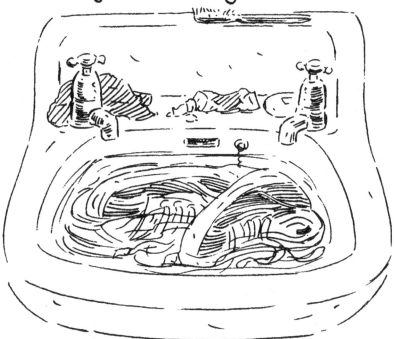

9·00am Sunday. Greg:
Put my trainers under my
bed last night. This morning
they were floating in the
washbasin.

2 am Monday.
Mrs M: Heard chains rattling under our bed in middle of the night. Nothing there when I looked with torch except some fluff. Must vacuum under there today.
9.30 pm Tuesday. Greg: Owl hooted in my school bag but nothing there when I looked.

The exercise book was left open on the sideboard and the ghosts began to read it to see if their hauntings had been noticed.

"Oh, look," said Scarem. "Mr Merry seems to have been very impressed by my scream through the letter-box."

"But not as much as Mrs Merry was by my dance of the black veils in front of the washing-machine," claimed Panic rather smugly.

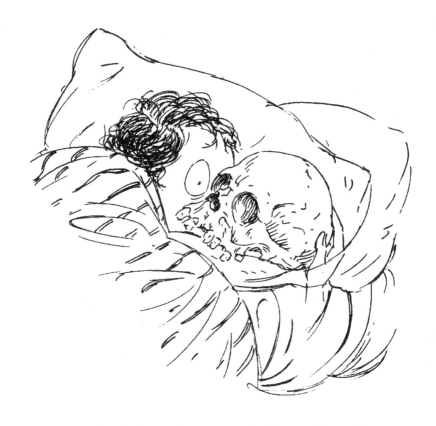

"And what about my skull on the pillow trick when Gregory woke up in the morning?" asked Gob.

"Not nearly as good as my moving the chair just as Joy was going to put her bottom on it," boasted Lin.

Slyly they began to compete to see who could get the most mentions in the exercise book and who could do the best haunting stunts. They even began (in a very glum kind of way, of course) to enjoy being so busy and mischievous all day and night. Because the

Merry family slept soundly they couldn't be haunted at night, so the O'Gools had to haunt them in the day, and slowly they began to get used to being awake in the daylight hours.

Chapter 8

The Merry family showed no signs of being in the least bit frightened by all these ghostly goings on. The children began to read books about ghosts, and in their untidy way left them open around the house. The ghosts were very interested to read about other spooks, spirits, spectres, wraiths, banshees, apparitions, phantoms and hobgoblins, and all the tricks they got up to. In fact the books gave them some great new ideas to try out on the Merry family.

Then Mrs Merry began to go to the local library to find out who had lived in the old house before them. She read a lot of ancient documents and registers and made notes. When she gathered her family together to tell them all about the people who had occupied the house before them they were fascinated. So were the O'Gools, who gathered invisibly in the room listening to every word.

"Now, I've found out from the old records that this house was built three hundred years ago," said Mrs Merry.

"Really? Who by?" asked her husband.

"A family of farmers called O'Gool. They had one boy who grew up here and took over the house when his father went to work at Castle Dire."

"That's me she's talking about!" exclaimed Scarem to his family. "And Grandfather O'Gool who worked as a coachman at the castle."

Mrs Merry consulted her notes. "Then this son married a rather dismal lady from the nearby village and they had two children."

"That's me!" said Panic.

"And us!" said the twins.

"They seem to have been an ordinary kind of farming family, though they weren't very popular locally."

"Why not?" asked Joy.

"Because they were such a grumpy lot, and the other villagers thought their miserable faces could turn the milk sour."

The O'Gools all looked at each other indignantly. "Humph!" said Scarem. "Slander!" said Panic.

"Then, unfortunately," Mrs Merry continued, "there was a terrible storm. They were all in the wood gathering mushrooms, and were hit by a thunderbolt – Bang! All dead, just like that!"

"Well, I never knew that!" said Scarem.

"So that's how we went. I always wondered," said his wife.

"After that nobody wanted to live in the house because they thought it was haunted by this O'Gool family. And I think they may have been right!" Mrs Merry concluded with a laugh. The Merry family and the O'Gools, side by side, had listened with great interest and now they all gave her a clap.

Later, back in the attic, Panic said, "You know, that Mrs Merry's an interesting woman in spite of her scrubbing everything clean all the time."

"And that Joy girl has got some very interesting computer games," admitted Gob.

Scarem looked at them sternly. "Now, you two, remember these people have invaded our home. We've been here for two hundred and fifty years and I'm not giving up now! They must be got rid of! I want you all to make a bigger effort."

Chapter 9

During the next few days, the O'Gools tried everything they could to scare the Merrys. Manacles shook, black sheets whisked in and out of rooms and the air was full of wails, toots, barks and howls. Bones seemed to be lying about everywhere and things moved almost as soon as they were put down.

The Merrys loved every minute of it.

The children began bringing friends home from school to stay the night. "Now you just listen for the dog or the owl or the chains rattling!" they'd warn their pals.

The ghosts performed more and more desperately in an effort to scare away the invading humans, so sure enough the visitors would hear a *twit-twoo!* from the wardrobe or a *woof! woof!* from behind the fridge. At night they would lie awake, thrilled to hear footsteps dragging overhead and the clanking of metal. The windows seemed to rattle all night long and the doors slammed every few minutes even though there wasn't a draught left in the house. Joy and Gregory became very popular at school as more and more people heard about their resident ghosts.

At last Scarem called another family conference in the attic.

"Look, I'm worn out with all this flitting about and haunting stuff," he said. "I'm also running out of ideas about what to do next. Any suggestions?"

"I'm quite enjoying it," admitted Panic, "but none of it seems to be scaring them one little bit, does it?"

"I'd like to go on haunting the kitchen if you don't mind, because the steam that comes off some of the food they cook is delicious," said Gob.

"Oh, yes! Did you smell that treacle pudding they had last night? Wasn't it divine!" Lin agreed.

"I must admit I'm beginning to prefer it to the scent of mildew myself . . . but that's not the point!" said Scarem angrily. "These people have taken over our home and we have to get rid of them. Now, how can we do it? Come on – think! Panic, what do you suggest?"

"Well, they seem to have got used to all our tricks, so what if we stopped doing anything at all for a fortnight and see what they'd do about that? They might just leave out of boredom."

"Boredom? The Merrys are never bored," said Gob.

"At least doing nothing would give us time to think up some new ideas," Lin suggested.

"All right, since we don't have any other ideas we'll give that one a try. No tricks for two weeks, everybody. Agreed?"

They all agreed.

Chapter 10

For two weeks no yowls, shrieks, whoops, clangs, boings, woofs or rattles were heard and no black wraiths or parts of skeletons were seen.

Joy and Gregory's friends were very disappointed. "I don't believe you've got ghosts at all, you're just making it up," they complained. They soon stopped asking for invitations to the house.

At the end of the first week Joy said to Gregory, "You know, I really miss all those noises and skulls and see-through figures, don't you?"

"Yes, I do. It's as if the house has gone dead. As if some friends have gone away," he agreed.

Mr Merry didn't like the quiet either. "Everything I've put down is exactly where I left it," he complained. "Screwdrivers, pencils and forks, the newspaper – absolutely nothing moves any more."

"And aren't the television programmes boring without a bit of background clatter and screeching! And I do miss seeing those

black figures nipping in and out of the walls all day long," said Mrs Merry with a sigh.

Even Felicity was bored now the owl no longer teased her by appearing and disappearing when she hunted in the wood, and the ghost dog didn't push her food dish under the washing-machine or bark in her ear when she took a snooze.

Over the evening meal they all agreed the house was a lot duller and they wished the ghosts would start their activities again.

At the end of the two weeks the O'Gools had another family conference in the attic.

"You know, I find this attic a bit chilly compared with the rest of the house," Scarem observed.

"And I'm ashamed how dusty it is," admitted Panic. "We'll give it a bit of a tidy up tomorrow."

238

"Fine, but that's not the point. We're here to review the battle against the Merry family," said Scarem. "Any observations? Gob?"

"It's been a very boring fortnight, and I don't think I enjoy boredom any more," said Gob.

"I agree. Flitting about in the graveyard and knocking on doors in the village is dull after you've done some real haunting," his sister agreed.

"I must admit I didn't know how to pass the time myself," Panic admitted, "so I followed Mrs Merry around. She reads some very interesting books – I had a glance through them when she put them down."

"And Mr Merry is very clever with his hands. It was quite fascinating watching him make a wooden seat for the garden," Scarem observed.

But then he remembered the Merrys were their enemies and they were still no nearer getting them out of the house. "The point is, a home once fit for ghosts to live in has been made uninhabitable!" he reminded his family.

"Well, has it, dear?" asked Panic. "After all, we *are* still inhabiting it."

"And some of those television programmes are very interesting," Gob added.

"And I've begun to understand how the computer games work by watching Joy and Gregory play them. They're great fun," said Lin.

"Felicity's really not as fierce as she looks, and I think she's a bit lonely with no other animals nearby," growled Dreary, and Howl tooted in agreement.

"What!" shouted Scarem. "Are my own family turning traitors? Don't you *want* these humans out and everything back to the lovely dreary way we had it before they invaded us?"

The other O'Gools shuffled their transparent feet and avoided his eye.

"This is terrible! Terrible!" said Scarem, stamping his foot (it went soundlessly through the floor) and storming off through the roof in a very bad temper.

"Never mind your father, dears," said Panic. "He'll be back when he's cooled down and had a think. Now shall we go down and have a sniff at the supper? I think they're having pizzas tonight followed by bread and butter pudding."

Chapter 11

The Merrys were still feeling rather glum without their hauntings.

"I do hope the ghosts haven't left us for good," said Mr Merry.

"Perhaps we've offended them in some way and they're giving us the cold shoulder. If we knew what we'd done we could apologize," said Mrs Merry.

"How could we ask them to start again?" wondered Gregory.

"I bet they can read, so why don't we leave a few notes lying about inviting them to haunt us again?" Joy suggested. Everyone thought this was a good idea. They made up this letter and left several copies lying around the house:

Dear O'Grools,

It's been a bit quiet lately! We hope you haven't left us, because we had a lot of laughs when you haunted us. Would you please start again as we have missed your company.

Best wishes, Yours sincerely,
Mr. Merry, Mrs. Merry
Joy, Gregory
and Felicity.

The O'Gools read the notes, of course, and Scarem called another of his family meetings in the attic. This was now much smarter as they'd swept the cobwebs and dust away and

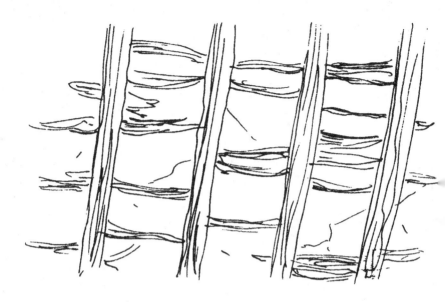

cleaned the window. It was almost as cheerful as the rooms downstairs.

"Now, what are we going to do about these notes?" he said. "I'd like to hear from you each in turn, starting with you, Panic."

"Well, I think we should go back to haunting the Merrys immediately. I realize now it will never frighten them, but I do enjoy doing it and they seem to appreciate our efforts, don't they?"

"Gob?"

"I agree. How we used to live before now looks very dull. Also I like Joy and Gregory and I'd like to make friends with them."

"Lin?"

"I think the same. It's fun playing tricks on them and their food is just delicious. I'll never

smell mildew and ditchwater ever again. Yuk!"

"Dreary and Howl?"

"Felicity's meaty chunks smell wonderful."

"And since she's been hunting in the wood there are lots more ghost mice for me to chase."

"So, you all seem to have made your minds up to live alongside these humans," observed Scarem. "Well, I've been thinking about it myself and I've come to the same conclusion. We shall never drive them out, and I'm not going to leave my home after two hundred and fifty years, so we seem to be stuck with each other."

His family cheered and clapped and howled their approval.

On the floor below, the Merrys were lying in their beds, but they sat up with big smiles on their faces when they heard the racket coming from above.

"Great! They're back," said Mr Merry and he fell happily asleep.

Chapter 12

From that day on the two families lived alongside each other very contentedly, though one was invisible to the other.

The O'Gools still moved things mischievously, but now they also moved them to help. When Mr or Mrs Merry was working in the kitchen the O'Gools would be there sniffing all the lovely ingredients and cooking smells, but also placing in position the next wooden spoon or saucepan or herb that would be needed. In the same way, Mr Merry always found his spanners or pliers conveniently to hand when he was doing repairs on the car or the house.

Gob and Lin spent many hours playing computer games with the two human children. They still played tricks on them but the four became very good friends. At night Joy and Gregory would settle down to read in their beds while nearby two books lay on the carpet with the pages turning over by themselves.

Downstairs the four grown-ups would be watching TV together, chuckling at the same jokes or cheering for the same football team. At meals the two families were together, one inhaling the lovely warm smells of the food and the other family eating it.

The O'Gools could never speak to the humans directly but the Merrys knew they were there and addressed some of their remarks to them. Sometimes they forgot and did this when visitors were there, which baffled them.

The O'Gools always helped to blow out the candles on the birthday cakes and now they knew what a "party" meant.

They even invited Grandfather O'Gool over for a ghost party they held in the attic and he smiled for the first time in three hundred years.

In summer the two families all piled into the Merrys' old car and went off for a picnic or a day by the sea. The ghosts came to enjoy sniffing flowers, sea air, chocolate, strawberries, grass and fish and chips.

Felicity looked sleek and fit. Dreary and Howl played hide and seek with her in the

woods and when they were all tired they
came back home to enjoy her meaty chunks,
she eating them and the other two sniffing
them. Dreary and Howl now slept in her
cupboard, though Felicity snored dreadfully.

The O'Gools sometimes helped to enter-
tain guests by putting on a haunting display,

howling and wailing, shimmering and knocking on windows as they used to do. The Merrys suggested a few new tricks they could try. It was noticeable though that their

haunting sheets were no longer black, but a rather fashionable yellow and green floral pattern which the O'Gools had copied from one of Mrs Merry's dresses.

And the biggest change of all was that the O'Gools had at last learned to laugh.

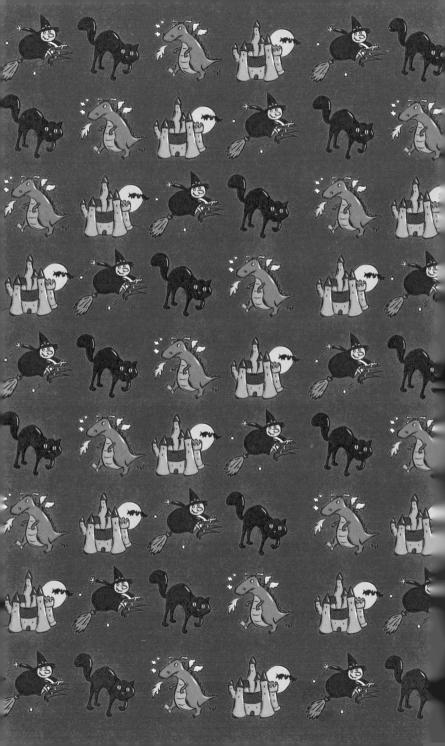